Margrit Cruickshank grew up in Scotland and studied languages
at Aberdeen University. In 1970 she moved to Ireland where her titles
Skunk and the Ozone Conspiracy and *A Monster Called Charlie*
were shortlisted for book awards, and in 1993, *Circling the Triangle*
won the Readers Association of Ireland Special Merit Award.
Margrit works part-time in a bookshop and lives in Dun Laoghaire
with her husband, three children and several cats.

Dave Saunders trained at Brighton Art College. He worked as
a primary school teacher for many years and is now a full-time
illustrator of children's books. Together with his wife Julie Saunders
he has created several young picture books for Frances Lincoln, including
The Ducks' Tale, The Ducks' Winter Tale, The Brave Hare and *The Big Storm*.
Dave lives in Malvern Link, Worcestershire.

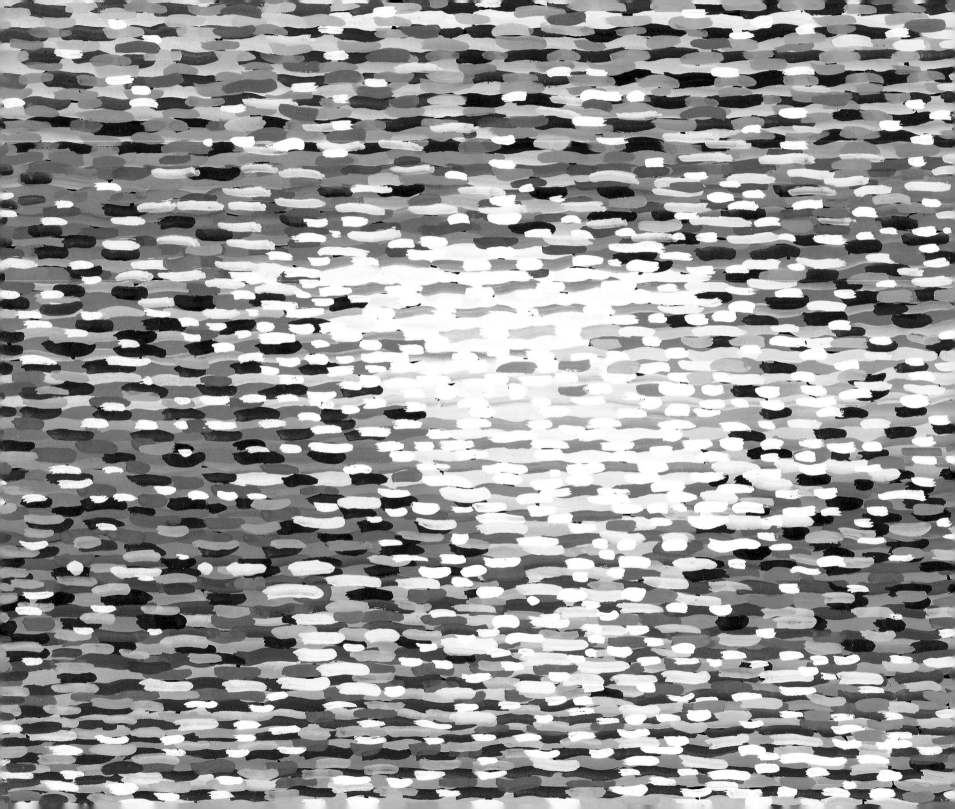

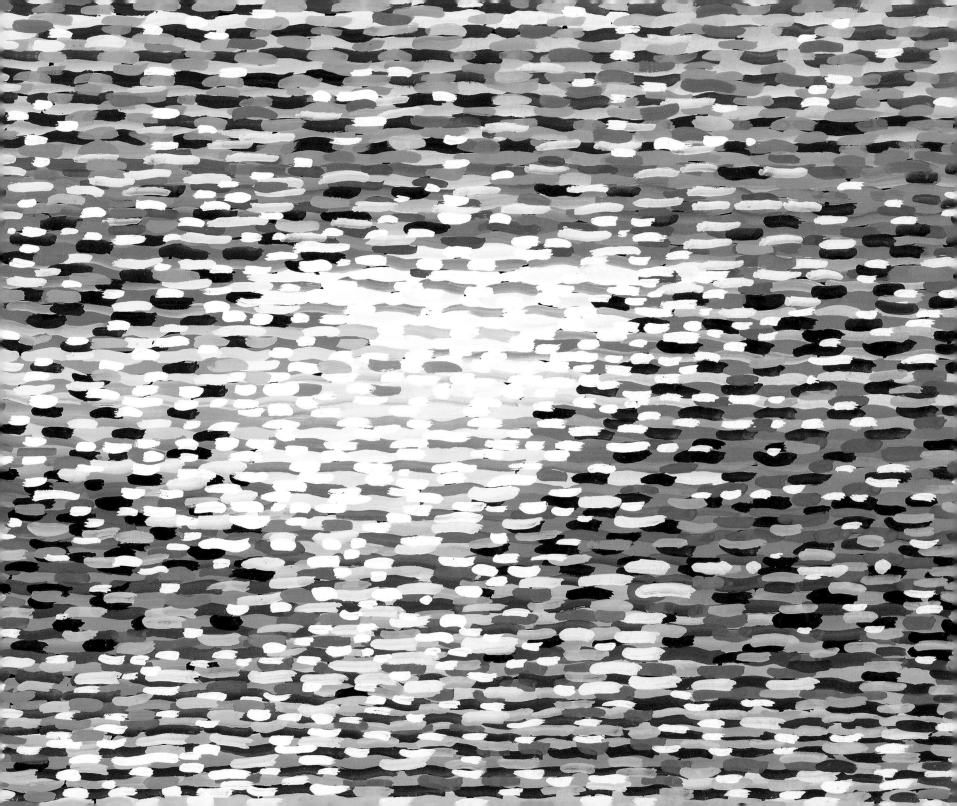

To Catriona, Andrew and Kirsten with love - *M.C.*
To Cyril Underwood - *D.S.*

First published in Great Britain in 1995 by
Frances Lincoln Limited, 4 Torriano Mews
Torriano Avenue, London NW5 2RZ

First paperback edition 1996

British Library Cataloguing in Publication Data
available on request

ISBN 0-7112-0977-4 hardback
ISBN 0-7112-0978-2 paperback

Printed and bound in Hong Kong

1 3 5 7 9 8 6 4 2

DOWN BY THE POND

A surprise farmyard book

Margrit Cruickshank & Dave Saunders

FRANCES LINCOLN

A red fox crept across the yard,
his black-tipped tail was twitching hard,
in the farmyard, down by the pond.

His tail twitched hard, for he heard the hens
clucking away in their wire net pens
(the henhouse was next to the pond).

The hens didn't know that the fox was there,
but the Jersey cow raised her head to stare
(she'd been drinking, down at the pond).

The cow raised her head and saw something slink past the sty of the pig (who was black and pink and lived very near to the pond).

The fox was seen (as he slunk through the farm) by the old collie dog, who rushed out of the barn and raced, barking, down to the pond.

The dog rushed out with a **yelp** and a **yap**,
while a little grey kitten was taking a nap
in the shade of a bush, by the pond.

She sat up in fright, the little grey kit,
then she narrowed her small green eyes to a slit
and stretched herself, down by the pond.
She narrowed her eyes, for she'd seen the twitch
of a hairy red tail with a pointy black tip...

Who do you think it belonged to?

MIAOW!

YOWL!

OINK!

WOOF!

MOO!

CLUCK!

The cat went "**Miaow!**"
and she pounced on the tail,

The fox went "**Yowl!**" with a shattering wail,

The pig went "**Oink!**"
as the fox leapt away,

The dog went "**Woof!**"
and joined in the fray,

The hens went "**Cluck!**"—

What a hullabaloo!

MIAOW!

YOWL!

OINK!

WOOF!

MOO!

CLUCK!

The pig went "**Oink!**"

The cat went "**Miaow!**"

The dog went "**Woof!**"

The fox went "**OW!**"

As the dog nipped his heels,

And the Jersey cow
lowered her head
and butted him.......

WOW!

He flew right into the pond!

"**Cluck!**" said the hens,
"that served him right!"

"**Oink!**" said the pig,
"I gave him a fright!"

"**Woof!**" said the dog,
"I scared him away!"

"**Moo!**" said the cow,
"I saved the day!"

But the little grey kitten, she winked a green eye
and went back to sleep in the sun by and by.

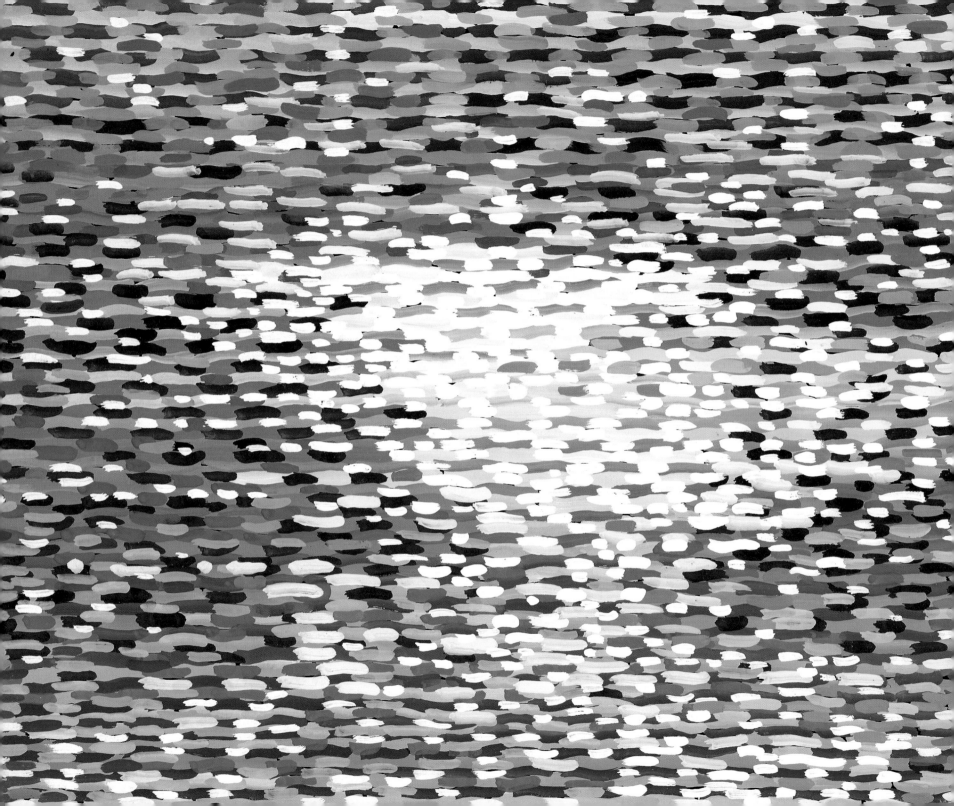

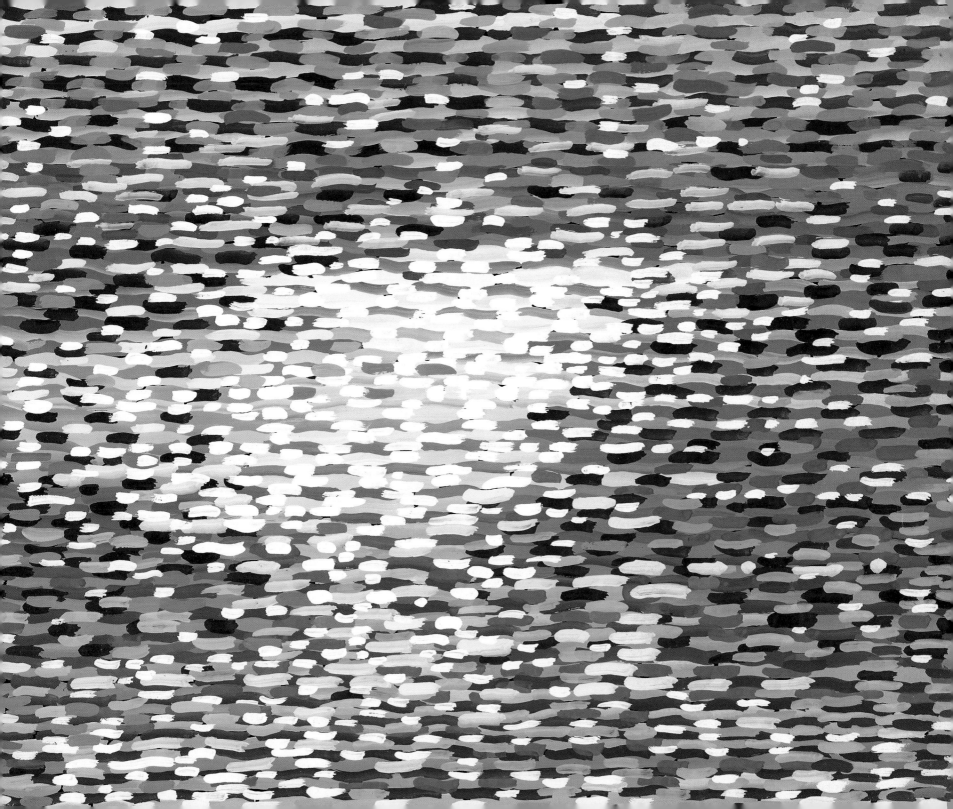

MORE PICTURE BOOKS IN PAPERBACK FROM FRANCES LINCOLN

THE BIG STORM
Dave and Julie Saunders

Dark clouds are gathering over the wood. "Hide and shelter!" cry the animals one by one, running into their holes and burrows. As the storm breaks, the Squirrels find an unlikely hiding-place and, when the rain stops, a surprise treasure-trove as well!

Suitable for National Curriculum English - Reading, Key Stage 1
(Scottish Guidelines, English Language - Reading, Levels A and B)

ISBN 0-7112-0865-4 £3.99

THE BRAVE HARE
Dave and Julie Saunders

Hare is hungry, and tells all his farmyard friends of his plan to feast among the cabbages. "Oh no. You can't do that!" they cry, and one by one they warn him of the terrible things he will find there. But tales of furious farmers, giants and monsters don't deter the brave Hare in the slightest - and he proves his well-meaning friends wrong...

Suitable for National Curriculum English - Reading, Key Stage 1
(Scottish Guidelines, English Language - Reading, Levels A and B)

ISBN 0-7112-0761-5 £3.99

RED FOX ON THE MOVE
Hannah Giffard

When a bulldozer tears apart the den of Red Fox and his family, they find themselves on the move. In their search for a new home, they encounter an angry snake and an owl. Finally, after taking refuge on a barge, they wake up in the city, where they find their perfect hole in a beautiful wild garden.

"Hannah Giffard is an original, the undiscovered talent publishers dream about." *The Bookseller*

Suitable for National Curriculum English - Reading, Key Stage 1
(Scottish Guidelines, English Language - Reading, Levels A and B)

ISBN 0-7112-0819-0 £3.99

All Frances Lincoln titles are available at your local bookshop or by post from:
Frances Lincoln Books, B.B.C.S., P.O. Box 941, Hull, North Humberside, HU1 3YQ.
24 Hour Credit Card Line 01482 224626
To order, send:
Title, author, ISBN number and price for each book ordered.
Your full name and address.
Cheque or postal order made payable to B.B.C.S. for the total amount, plus postage
and packing as below.
U.K. & B.F.P.O. - £1.00 for the first book, and 50p for each additional book up to
a maximum of £3.50.
Overseas & Eire - £2.00 for the first book, £1.00 for the second and 50p for each additional book.

Prices and availability are subject to change without notice.